W9-BNT-309

WINTER
Tracks in the Snow

by *Janet McDonnell*
illustrated by Linda Hohag

created by Wing Park Publishers

CP CHILDRENS PRESS®
CHICAGO

Library of Congress Cataloging-in-Publication Data

McDonnell, Janet, 1962--
    Winter : tracks in the snow / by Janet McDonnell ; illustrated by
Linda Hohag.
        p.   cm. — (The Four Seasons)
    "Created by Wing Park Publishers"
    Summary: While searching for a friend to have winter fun with,
Mouse follows the tracks of many animals in the snow, eventually
ending at Ground Hog's hole.
    ISBN 0-516-00679-7
    [1. Mice—Fiction.   2. Animal tracks—Fiction.   3. Winter—Fiction.
4. Ground Hog Day—Fiction.]   I. Hohag, Linda, ill.   II. Title.   III.
Series: McDonnell, Janet, 1962-   Four seasons.
PZ7.M1547Wi   1993
[E]—dc20   93-20172
                                                              CIP
                                                               AC

WINTER
Tracks in the Snow

It was a cold, winter morning in the forest. All was quiet. Under the ground, nine mice were asleep in their burrow. But one mouse was awake.

"I'm bored," he said. "All we do is sleep and eat. I want to go out and look for fun." He nudged his friend and said, "Hey, want to come with me?"

"Mmmm, no way. It's nice and warm in here," said his friend.

"Well, I'm out of here," said Mouse.

When he poked his head outside, Mouse
could barely keep his eyes open. He was not
used to the bright, white snow. "Wow! It's
beautiful!" he said. He ran and jumped
through the cold, fluffy powder until he was
out of breath.

Then he looked around him. He had left
squiggly tracks everywhere. That gave Mouse
an idea. I'll look for other tracks and follow
them, he thought. Maybe they will lead to
a friend!

Mouse followed the first tracks he could find. They led him into the woods. Mouse couldn't believe his eyes. "The trees!" he cried. "They're all dead!"

"They're not dead, silly," said a voice.

Mouse looked around. Behind one of the trees, he saw a young deer with his mother. "When spring comes, the trees will have a whole bunch of brand new leaves. My mama said so," said the young deer.

"Oh, that's a relief," said Mouse. "Hey, I followed your tracks right to you! Do you want to play?"

"I'm sorry, Mouse," said the mama deer,
"but he can't play now. We are busy looking
for food."

"Yeah, and it's hard work in the winter,"
said the little deer. "Snow covers the acorns

and other good stuff, and most of the plants
have stopped growing. Sometimes we have
to eat bark. Yuk! I like grass and apples
better."

"Well, good luck," said Mouse. "I'm going
to follow these new tracks."

Mouse followed the tracks as they twisted and turned through the woods. They led to the bottom of a big tree. Mouse looked around, but there were no more tracks. Then he spotted a hole in the tree trunk. "Aha!" he said. "Whoever made these tracks must be in that hole! HELLO IN THERE!" he called. There was no answer.

"I KNOW YOU'RE IN THERE!" he
shouted. But still no answer. Mouse picked
up a pine cone and threw it into the hole.
"OUCH!" said a voice.

13

A very angry squirrel poked his head out. "Hey, what's the big deal!" he said.

"I'm sorry," said Mouse. "I followed your tracks. I'm looking for someone to play with."

"Well I don't want to play. I want to sleep!" said Squirrel. "The only reason I leave this nest is to look for the acorns I buried last fall. It's too cold to play!" Before Mouse could say anything, Squirrel had disappeared back into the hole.

"Boy, he sure wakes up cranky," said Mouse.

Mouse wandered along, looking for more tracks. Suddenly, he stopped. He saw something strange. It stood up tall like a person, but it had no legs. It was wearing a hat and scarf, but it had sticks for arms. Mouse decided to have a closer look.

He looks friendly, thought Mouse, but what is he? "Nice day out, isn't it?" said Mouse. But the white thing didn't answer.

Then Mouse noticed that there were footprints all around the creature. "Hey, how did you make these tracks without any feet?" he asked. But again there was no answer. "Aw, you're no fun," said Mouse, hurrying away.

Maybe I'll find some tracks by the pond, Mouse thought. But when he got there, everything looked different. "What happened?" he cried. "The pond is gone!"

"No, it's not. It's just frozen," said a cardinal from a tree overhead. "The top of the water has turned to ice. Try it."

"Ice?" said Mouse. "Well, let's see..." He took two steps, then his paws slid across the ice. He spun around and landed with a thump on his bottom. "I don't think I like ice," he said.

"Hey, what about the fish?" Mouse asked. "How do they swim in ice?"

"Only the top of the water is frozen," said Cardinal. "The fish stay at the bottom of the pond. They barely move, and they don't eat. They just wait for spring to come."

"Everyone seems to be waiting for spring," said Mouse. "But not me. I'm tired of just waiting. I'm looking for fun! Hey, there are some more tracks! Bye, Cardinal!" And off he went.

"Hmmm, these look like hopping tracks," said Mouse. He followed them toward a big evergreen. Sure enough, he could see Hare hiding under the tree.

"Why, Hare! You have a new white coat!" Mouse called in surprise. "Where did you get that?"

"Shhh, not so loud," said Hare. "I'm hiding.
And you better hide too!"

"Why should I hide?" asked Mouse.

"Because there are lots of hungry hunters
around," said Hare. "Like Owl and Fox.

"That's why my coat changed color. Each fall, I start to lose my old grey hair and grow white hair. Then I blend in with the snow better, so I'm harder to see."

Mouse looked down at his own grey coat. "I'm n-n-not afraid," he said. But inside, Mouse was scared. Maybe it's time to go back to the burrow, he thought.

"Be careful!" said Hare.

Mouse ran as fast as he could from bush to bush. But soon he came to a clearing. There was nothing to hide him. Now Mouse was worried. Suddenly, he had an idea. "I will tunnel my way home!" he cried.

He dove under the snow and tried running through the light powder. "This is fun!" he said. But then THUMP! He bumped his head on something big. It was a boot!

Mouse poked his head out of the snow. He was surrounded by people! Big ones and small ones, all standing around a hole in the ground. "Hey!" said Mouse, "that's Ground Hog's hole! They must be trying to catch Ground Hog!"

Mouse didn't have time to be afraid. He had to save his friend! In a flash, he zipped down the hole. "Ground Hog! Ground Hog!" he cried.

Ground Hog was just waking up. He stretched and gave a big yawn. "Well, hello, Mouse," he said. "What are you doing here? I was just thinking about going up for some food."

"No!" screamed Mouse. "You can't! There are people up there, waiting to catch you!"

Ground Hog just laughed. "Oh, Mouse, don't worry. This happens every year," he said.

"What happens?" asked Mouse.

"Every year, about this time, I start to get hungry. So I wake up from my long nap and go out to look for food. Because of this, the people have named a day after me. And my day is today! The people say that if I see my shadow today, it will scare me back into my hole, and that will mean a longer winter. But if I don't see my shadow, spring will come early. I know it's silly. But you know how people are."

"Well, I sure hope you don't see your shadow," said Mouse. "Because I'm tired of winter!"

"Follow me and find out," said Ground Hog. Mouse followed Ground Hog and peeked out of the hole. Just as Ground Hog walked onto the field, the sun went behind a cloud. There was no shadow. "Hooray!" the people all cheered. So did Mouse.

"Bye, Ground Hog," he said. "I'm going to tell all my friends back in the burrow that spring is coming!" And he tunnelled all the way home.

You have read what Mouse does in the winter.
Here are some things children do.

Can you read these words?

go ice skating

go sledding

make Christmas cookies

hang stockings

make a snowman

Can you think of other things?